Tedzells:

Poems &

Short Stories

Tedzells: Poems and Short Stories

Author: Andre Johnson

Translated by: Tanyaakkari (Spain)

Discount Code: books

10% Off Order

https://www.etsy.com/shop/Tedzells

Table of Content

Poems

Short Stories

Hippies Drinking Whiskey

The free one's soul that roams the earth

Relax in nature till end of birth

To the peaceful warriors that seek the sights of freedom

To the ones that free themselves from what's not needed

They find their whiskey and drink it up

Anyone who wants some, pour em a cup!

Cause they can't find the green leafs that they want

Can't harvest the soil, can't what's sold

Whiskey takes the edge off for the lack of what I can't smoke

So grab a bottle and drink till you can't think

Ease down, bottoms up! Nothing ever las forever

So close your eyes and dream of sativa

For someday you'll find it and smoke all day

And all your worries will go away

But for now just relax, we drink and chill

To remember the taste of indica and how the smoke
bends

So swallow these tasteful spirits and forget about it
all!

Wash our worries away with tasty alcohol

We struggle so much to find the precious weed

So we turn to our whiskey during these times of
need

Do anything to get that most coveted pot

So raise your glass and drink up!

Fill my cup and drink all that you've got!

Until we find some weed or delicious edibles.

A Childless Uncle

What were you doing last night? Sleeping.

Oh, I was up all night peeping

Into little Johnny's room.

He was crying all night, I assume?

Yes, I am tired and would love to go to bed,

How about we go out today? It's Friday. Let's grab
a drink instead?

I can't. I am busy taking care of my kid.

I have to swaddle, put to sleep and feed.

I see… well doesn't seem like a good night's rest,

Guess I'll go alone. Take a shower, get dressed,

Hit the town!

Party, drink, sing and dance till dawn.

Wake up at noon? Sure, do some yoga or sports,

Some physical activities of sorts?

On Monday I will be working,

But after that some Netflix, a bit of Reddit lurking,

On Tuesday I have my improv class.

Sorry what now? I had to wipe little Johnny's ass...

I'm saying that my schedule is pretty much full,

Mine too, but everything around the kid is exhausting and dull.

I have piano lessons. I learn German too,

I make my own schedule so I have only fun things to do,

I nearly forgot! Next week I and auntie are going skiing,

In the Alps! And Europe sightseeing,

It's going to be hell of trip,

Great food and fine wine... sip after sip,

After that back to work, finish up some stuff,

Finalize the project that looked a bit tough,

But that will certainly get me a raise,

It's good to have a job that both satisfies and pays,

After that, who knows? I got time on my hands,

I can do anything as it stands,

So, what are YOU doing tomorrow? Cause I'll be sleeping,

Oh... I will be up all night. Keeping

An eye on little Johnny in his room.

Tough life being a parent I presume.

And it sucks you be you.

Convenient Courage

I strive for more, the fear I must face.

My vision stays clear even while it rains.

Knowing my purpose gives me courage to grow.

The bottom of the mountain was all I used to know.

Every step I take I learn to take more.

My destination is promised, I feel it in my core.

My heart beast fast, I feel it go.

When adversity came I never ran.

Pain doesn't last, looking at my scars from my past.

If I stay the course, "what if's" won't be asked.

Tomorrow is not promised so I do what I can.

Close to attaining greatness, I'm right at the cusp.

So to strive for more, I must face the fear.

Even through the rain, my vision is clear.

Knowing my purpose gives me courage to grow.

The bottom of the mountain was all I used to know.

Shh, I Work Here

Shh, I work here!

I know my job title and I follow most of the rules

So you don't get to come here and try to me look
like an absolute fool!

I'm here day and night, to earn my pay check

And you're making it seem like I isn't shit

Shh, I work here!

Stop with all these complaints

I don't think you're a saint!

We all make mistakes; we're human just like you

You don't even know what we go through!

Shh, I work here!

Please don't come back!

I'm tired of all your stupid faces!

I smile politely though all your crap.

But in truth I don't ever want to see you again!

Shh, I work here!

You should have good manners.

Don't be so dense and heavy like a hammer.

See me as a person, treat me politely.

I'll gladly help you if you ask me nicely.

Shh, I work here!

And sure, you're welcome

If you're in need of the goods and service we can provide it.

But please don't be rude, please be nice.

Because being a kind person does not have a price.

Shh, I work here!

Customers are horrible!

Everyday interaction, I hope they go well.

Though their terrible behavior, I wanna punch stuff.

But I treat them well because I don't want to get fired!

Toilet Paper Math

Toilet Paper Math! Everyone says they're the best!

So let's crack this code open and put it to the test...

If one roll has a thousand, two have double as much

Is that what makes them feel so soft to the touch

The double of six thousand for the count of twelve

But they don't look so big up there on the shelves...

Then thirty six mega equals one hundred and forty four

The math is just not there

At least that's what I think I read at the store...

Toilet paper numbers that double and triple

One second, wait, they have how many plies?

So twenty four mega is like forty eight regular ones

I get double as much? How truly spectacular!

Then that only means you're getting more for the price

More bang for my buck! How awesome! Very nice!

Twenty four rolls those are actually twenty eight

So regular is double? I can't keep them straight!

And for only four rolls I get four thousand sheets

I could count them all as I'm warming the seat!

More sheets! More paper!

Damn! I'm all out...

I'll make my way to the store and go get some

Because toilet paper math ain't mathing right!

Hood Traumas

Living in the shadows of struggle, pushing through
the mantle of strife

Learning from the hustle, surviving every day
through the harshness of life

These tough surroundings that stunt our growth

And instill a deep fear for all things we loathe

The empty gun barrels, the betrayal of our youth

Silencing the words that hide the essence of our
truth

Harvest the tears of children; lose sight of what's
real

Anything to soothe the deep terror that they feel

The horrors of the street marked forever in their
skin

Wishing that one day they'll be absolved of all their
sins

Constant howling of wolves, the noise and echoes
of pain

Feeling like their efforts are all wasted and in vain

Safety and security are nothing but myths

And there's no one but you to share this madness
with

Distrust ingrained in the roots of all the people

Carefully aware of those abusing tipple

Endlessly chasing the calm after any storms

Seeking for a place where they'll be safe and warm

The repetitive motions of corrupted thoughts

Slowly spoiling our nature until everything rots

The young that follow blindly the path of their big homie

Hoping to find some warmth to take them through the winters

A life of glory, a path of stories, a debt to be paid

A woeful trade of a soul that's been made to kill and obey

Never question the words of their fellow men

Respond to all their orders no matter where and when

Escape from all the chains that will hold them back

Mentally suffer as they prepare for the attack

Defend themselves from all outside danger

Cause their mothers taught them to never trust a stranger

To turn their cheek and come back home

To be wary and ignore all those who may roam

Darkness and dusk that swallow every corner

Psychos that wander about disrupting all the order

The cloud of sorrow overshadowing it all

Catching anyone who stumbles and falls

No mercy, no rest – wickedness galore

Grow up as you ignore the blood that stains the
floor

Dirty pavement, untold crimes, and unjust victims

All a part of the same cursed, broken system

There's people working hard to keep us all down

Up on the TV and they're smiling as we frown

But the cogs are turning and the world is young

There will be a time when they'll swallow their
tongue

And pay their debt to the song of the end

And by then we'll discover whose foe and whose
friend.

Black Air Force Fibs

One shoe is forever a classic

Some use them to hoop, some view as ratchet

Black Air forces are always in style

Sometimes creased with the star on the bottom

Nobody wants problems when you have these
things on

Keep my laces tied because I am always on the
grind

No matter the weather, mines always stay on

Black forces will stay classics

Don't mess with a person in all black forces

Forget what you saw or you'll have a long ass night

Not to be trusted and very quick to react

Thief in the night comes with the strap

You can tell by the crease this man don't play

Been walking for miles, might find where you stay

Stomping the curb, maybe kicking some rocks

Kicked down some doors and jumped some fences

Best not to stop, be cool when they pass

Black air force is like boot to ass

Don't care bout nothing, he stick to the streets

You can tell by the shoes on their feet

Don't mess with a person in all black forces

So forget what you saw or have a long as night

Not to be trusted and very quick to react

A thief in the night normally wears black forces

Christmas Movies

Is it based off Saint Nick, or a jolly fat man?

Does it put you in the spirt of given?

Is the plot around Christmas and filled with snow?

Only one question can explain:

Is there a Christmas movie plot?

Real world parties have,

Secret Santa and Pizza Parties in the breakroom

Christmas movies shindigs

Held in Japanese named Nakatom

Most parties have a lot of drinking and dancing

But a real good movie deals with Germans and ransoms'

If any trouble comes about the cop get called

But in a real Christmas Movie we have

John McClane

Therefore I Say:

Yippee Ki-Yay

Military Problems

Through different dirt's of the world

A trail is formed

By restless footsteps

Marching their way home

Why is it?

That the world never seems to run out of reasons:

Reasons to send their soldiers away

Reasons to not have them come back

Reasons to not help them once they do

Reasons to send them away once more.

The trail of their dirt-covered feet is beaten

And the blood is hardened on their soles

And faces

And the scars they bare run deep,

Deeper than any layer of skin.

Their hearts are stuck

Beating in rhythm with the explosion of gunfire

A world away.

Words get stuck in their throats

As they try to bring them up

The lost hearts and dreams

Of the fallen.

Why the world is covered in song

And celebration?

Who thinks of the soldiers?

Gasping for breath

Still stuck in their march

Their hands forever-glued to their guns

And their eyes to their surroundings,

As there's no longer a place that's safe

From the war that covers the world.

Overqualified

The weight of the world is carried by one.

Many will look, few will come.

Days will pass and I will continue to get stronger.

Staying in motion, I can wait no longer.

When times are though, I have to rely on me.

Paid the cost the price was steep.

The motivation I have is fueled by me.

Let down too many times, I took control of the keys.

The road is long but I'm up to the task.

The faith in myself is all I have.

I will keep pressing on till I get the path I want.

Even if help is not given.

The weight of the world is carried by one.

Many will look, few will come.

Days will pass and I will continue to get stronger.

Staying in place, I can't wait no longer.

No

No is a wonderful word.

It should be said a lot more than yes.

No matter where you are in the world it has the
same meaning.

This word No, is so great.

Even saying the word no can save your mental
health.

Don't believe me, let's try it out

Want to go to a party?

No.

Can I borrow some money?

Hell no.

Can you watch my children?

Fuck them kids

All the same meaning.

After all, you're the only one taking care of

Your mental health.

A Soldiers War

Jack was a very popular Sergeant back in the army, known for his cunning mind and ruthless spirit. Although after the war was over and both him and the privates under him returned to the real world, his popularity declined. After spending 10 years in a never ending war, he knew that he was a mighty soldier and could handle anything that was ordered, but he was not used to crowded bar where anyone could flank him. He was not used to getting drinks in the late night; alcohol would make his hands shaky. Girls? He barely had any time to think about them, he prioritized survival over anything.

He was sent to a foreign country with his friends in the army. He was the only survivor of a big ambush and that was the first bullet into his mind, being the only one left in the whole draft. He was tortured for many days until he got rescued, but the real thing was being alone; whippings or deep cuts that made him bleed couldn't touch his soul, but not being able to protect his comrades really hurt his heart. The second bullet happened in his 3rd year. He stopped receiving letters from his wife back in the U.S for a while, but he was a patient man. He knew that his wife and newborn left at home were curious about him. They would wait for him, as he would wait to return to them, dreaming about them each night. The latest letter he received that year was about legal papers, regarding that his wife now wanted a divorce.

He was sad, but didn't really have time to think about it. He couldn't process what happened in his mind because of the gunfire and constant need of protection. Third bullet was perhaps the most keen one. He received a letter in his 5th year this time, and it was about reporting a traffic accident; where he lost his so-called ex-wife and his precious little daughter, Lily. He was going through tough times, but no one knew it. Even he didn't know much about the storm in his heart. He would eat, work out, grab his gun and go for another day; to protect his comrades as much as he could, as he had no one else to do.

Again, after ten years of constant battling and he returned home, he realized that all of his privates were happy to meet their families. They hugged their daughters and sons; their wives unleashed tears of joy. He was happy about the scene; he really enjoyed seeing his friends happy and whole as a family. No one went to see him, but he didn't care anyway and led to the house that the military provided for him. He entered the room which resembled a cheap motel. The first thing he did was to lock the door and put something behind it to blockade. Then he removed his uniform and took a hot bath. He realized how many scars he had on his body that day, and it was way more than he imagined. He then got out of the shower and sat on top of the bed. He stood still for a while. He didn't know what he would do. He stared at the blank wall in front of him for an hour or so.

He realized that his eyes were hurting, but he didn't know why. "I had enough food. I had enough sleep. No wind was in sight and the weather was clear." he said to himself, couldn't understand the logic behind the pain. He tried to sleep on the bed with his handgun next to him but no matter how much he tried, he couldn't fall asleep. He pushed the pillows aside, changed his position, and checked the handgun and its magazine multiple times. He couldn't sleep. He got up and started doing push-ups. 50, 51, 52… What would be his next step? He knew nothing but war; he knew nothing but how to battle. 124, 125, 126… What was the meaning of the Medal of Honor he got, if he no longer could protect the lives of other soldiers, risking their lives at the battlefield? 203… 204… 205…

He took another hot shower and felt blissful. "Two hot ones a day. Happens once a lifetime." he murmured. He thought it would be a fine joke to tell to the boys, without realizing that he wouldn't see them again, not as he thought. He then tried to sleep again, but this time he didn't touch the bed. He lay on the hard, concrete floor and it felt way, way better. He thought about his new life again, and he

fell asleep shortly after.

Work Spouse

This story begins like many before but I'll begin with the basics. I am 32 years old I was raised in the Bible belt southern states and was raised as such. I learned at a young age of the importance of monogamy and all that jazz. I have also been married for 10 years and have two kids with my wife whom I love dearly. My name though is John I come from good Scottish stock. I am 5 feet 10 inches tall carry a little bit of weight and am of working class. I'm not gonna lie to you and tell you how well-endowed I am, I am just a slightly above average guy with about 6 inches and the sex drive of a teenager still.

See I did it all how I was supposed to. I finished high school, went to college and then entered the workforce. My job is adrenaline filled which has always been good for me because I am an adrenaline junkie. After 7 years though the adrenaline started to fade. I lost interest and wanted to find that rush again. I also met my work wife, she is great and beautiful. Isabel is also 5 feet 10 inches and she has curves in the right places. We started off with flirtatious picking, and then became good friends. She always respected the bounds of my marriage and although hinting at liking me further it never felt like there was a push.

To say we had become close was a minor understatement. I knew details of her life that most would not and vice versa. That being said, I knew that she needed to look elsewhere to work. My workplace does not pay very well. With that said I had to carry on a long distance work wife relationship. Most would think that is bad, but that is just where my story takes an interesting twist.

You see Isabel only had to move and hour and a

half away and the longer she was gone the steamier

the conversations got. I would often when I was

home alone pull my member out and stroke it to

thoughts of conversations we had and how I would

love to cum deep inside her. See my dream is that I

could become a polygamist and my wife and I could

just welcome Isabel into our home and marriage.

One day we were talking about a look she

gives and a picture that I often use in my fantasies.

She sent me a different picture that was better and

asked if this is the one. I said no but told her how

this one was amazing. It is of her lying on the floor

in a tank top and her ample breast almost spilling

out of the tank top. The look in her eyes is just

begging me to fuck her, needless to say I whipped

my dick out and rubbed one out. This photo was the key though, it was the key to better photos because I was able to let Isabel know about how I felt. This lead to me receiving a photo with her tits out and covered by her hand, all except for a small part of her nipple. I went wild and I could hear the way she has always jokingly called me daddy and my dick got so hard it was ready to burst. From that moment we began sharing risky photos to include some that are completely nude but with some editing.

I could no longer take it though, all this teasing made me need some of that pussy. I asked and Isabel was down, so we set up a time to meet. I had a meeting at work that was canceled, so we decided I would drive down to her house. She had left the door unlocked and I walked on in. The bedroom was lit with candles, flickering in the dark room. The flame inspired light licked Isabel's body painting a picture that can only be described as a pornographic expressionist painting, like a Monet that no art museum will show. The matching black lingerie accented her curves perfectly, making her already beautiful breast are perkier and her curve at her waist more pronounced. The room smelled of vanilla, roses and sandalwood, all fresh and creating an intoxicating scent. The entire experience already had my head swimming and my dick pulsing with my heartbeat.

Isabel got off the bed and sauntered over to me. She made quick work of getting my clothes off, taking a hold of my cock and giving me our first kiss ever. It was a sensual French Kiss, just the right amount of tongue. I reciprocated with a show of what I had intended to do to her pussy before we fuck. As I did so Isabel was softly stroking my hard cock and let out a soft moan. She moved to her knees and began to suck my dick. Her skills were phenomenal and I was ready to blow within 10 minutes. I am normally not a quick finisher. I told her I was about to cum and she just kept sucking. Then she pulled my cock from her mouth, told me she wanted me to cum at least twice. She began to lick just behind the head on the underside of my cock and I burst into her mouth. I came so hard in her mouth and she took it all and swallowed my seed.

I put her on her bed and ripped her bra and underwear off of her. I began to kiss him still tasting the slightly salty taste of my seed on her breath. I moved down and took those two amazing tits in my hands. I began at the base of one with a gentle bite, moving up to the top where I teased and nipped at the nipple then finally sucking it in and flicking the tip with my tongue. I traded off between breast teasing and nipping.

The entire time I had also been rubbing my quickly hardening dick against Isabel's ample wet pussy. I could feel her juices flowing and could tell that I was leaking precum. I moved down between her legs where I gently began kissing and nipping at Isabel's inner thighs. I moved all the way into the crease of her thigh licking. If I had not been intoxicated by the scent of the room I was most certainly intoxicated by the scent of her sex. It was a sweet and spicy smell comparable to the roses that grow beside my house. Not the scent you are used to associating with roses, no this one is still sweet but with a wild side. I moved into the lips of her pussy and began to kiss it. I started with the gentle sucking of light pecks. I then began to nibble on her lips and suck them into my mouth. I ran my tongue from her perineum to her clit, stopping there to French kiss her clit. I could hear her breathing get more intense and she just began to softly moan again. This time though she was also muttering "oh my God yes! Fuck I have never felt anything like this!"

She was begging for more so I slid two fingers into her pussy and began to fuck her while still making out with her clit. I could feel her pussy contracting on my finger and I just kept going. Finally I turned my fingers in her pussy and drove them deep in finding the little pressure pocket just below the cervix, I began rubbing that with my fingertips while my knuckles continued to hit her g spot and my tongue and mouth were on her clit. Basically she began riding my face as she had an orgasm.

I moved up to be face to face with Isabel who at this point had melted into the bed, I kissed her once more reminding her of how I had just eaten her pussy and then I knelt between her thighs. I began to rub my cock at the entrance of her wet pussy

. I would put the tip in then slide it out and up rubbing her clit. She shuddered then when she wasn't expecting it, I slid my cock all the way in. I could feel the tip resting where my fingers had previously been and with slow, short, hard strokes I pushed my cock right into that area below the cervix. Isabel breathed deep and her pussy clenched down again this time on my cock and it began to pulse. She was now just repeating a mantra of "oh shit, oh shit, oh shit, gimme that dick. Fuck fucknfuck oh MY GOOOODDDD"! It was at this point I pulled halfway out shifted my angle and began to fuck her so that my cock head was rubbing her g spot again. I did this with a quick pace and as she rolled into this orgasm, I felt a small rush of liquid that was very slick and I realized she had just ejaculated a bit. I was very thankful I had cum once already because it definitely prolonged the experience.

I pulled out of her my cock still throbbing, she said she wanted me to cum and that I could cum anywhere I wanted. I told her I wanted to fuck her in doggie and she got up on all fours. I looked at the beautiful pussy and ass in front of me and drove my cock into her pussy. I began to fuck Isabel with everything I had left and I could tell an orgasm was not far away. I pounded and pounded and watched as her asshole began contracting. This gave me an idea so I lubed up my left pointer finger with her ample juices and stuck my finger in her ass. She began to cum hard and I was about to burst so I kept pushing and finally I slid my finger out, grabbed her hips and buried my cock as far as I could into her. I came inside her pussy and the way she was contracting I knew where that seed was headed. I pulled my cock out and she slowly rolled over. She then told me she was not on the pill or any birth control. I told her I guess we will have to see what happens.

Off My Grass

Brian was the manager of a company and the one thing he hated more than anything else was that people would walk on different areas of the grass. He loved when grass was untouched and beautiful with all of the work done to it. When people walked all over it they seemed to destroy it and no matter how many times he would walk outside and tell people to stop walking on the grass they would never listen. He even had an entire staff meeting and fought hard in order to be able to install a do not walk on the grass sign out in the front.

It didn't seem to really do anything though because people ignored the signs they still ended up walking over his damn grass. He needed a new plan and this one he knew that he was going to do, even if he would get sued. He had thought very hard about what to do because he wanted to keep people off of the grass. While at the same time damaging the grass and losing his damn mind. It took a few tries and half dozen beers. Nonetheless he finally finished installing his latest invention.

He had managed to rewire an electric dog fence so that any person that stepped onto the grass would activate the sensor and get a small shock. It wouldn't pick up anything very light like animals because while he hated them being on the grass he knew that they didn't understand he wanted them off of it. He even tested the fence on himself and stepped on his own grass onto to get a massive shock. He sat near a window and watched the first day waiting for somebody to ignore the signs he had put up and step onto the grass.

It only took a few minutes and by noon several people had come asking to speak to the manager. They would tell him they got shocked, and he would just shrug and tell them that the sign said to stay off of the grass. In the afternoon a group of young adults came towards the building and Brian recognized them. They were known for coming around often and were the people he hated the most.

He constantly had to kick them off of the grass and they would step on it just to bother him. They would even pick at the grass and leave garbage on it to bother him. He was very excited to see their reactions to getting a shock from his new system. They went on the grass when they saw Brian was watching and jumped back when they got shocked from the system and looked right at the window surprised to see Brian standing there, watching, and laughing. He opened his mouth and the same words they heard him say a million times before came out.

"Stay off of the fucking grass."

Save the Sheep

Some Aliens heard the government. They heard us when we tried to contact them and when we tried to invite them earth. Unfortunately for us, they were impressed with our technology or our math, they were impressed by the damage we did to our planet, and to each other. Soon after they received our first signal, they started watching us.

After years and years of watching the Earthlings, some aliens finally decided to attack our planet. It wasn't an easy decision at first. Because they didn't need any more plants, but they made a list of the horrible things that we did to our planet an though we concerned for less. They tried seeing the good too, but the condition of our planet was in and made them feel like we were not worthy of it. They spend a year preparing and perfecting their ways of attacking, being prepared for any response. They figured out how exactly our stuff on Earth worked, so they knew what to prepare for everything. The only ones they wanted to spare were the children and the animals because they are innocent creatures.

They decided that they will educate the children of the plant, to be better humans than the generations before. They wanted to help humans to love themselves and their planet again. The planet needed some help, as the pollution got worse over the years, and the planet was getting sicker and sicker by the day. Even though they decided to attack the Earth, they didn't visit it much. They only used technology to watch us humans and anime. So they decided to visit one last time before they attacked.

"Let's be sure that we don't make a mistake," said the head of the operation, "We want to help them, not be like them," he added. They spread all around the world, in rich and poor countries, in cities and villages, making sure to check everything. They tried going to many different places, seeing all kinds of different people, so they could make the right decision. One of the searching troops ended up in a small village, somewhere deep in the countryside. On a big green meadow, there was a man with his sheep. The aliens approached, as they saw the farmer pushing a baby sheep into the water, or so they thought.

"What are you doing there, farmer?" Asked one of the bog eyed aliens. The form that they presented themselves as was always a human, perfectly fitted for where they were. Their form changed automatically considering the planet they were on. So now, the aliens looked like two men from the countryside, two farmers. "Why are you trying to drown that sheep?" Asked the other alien angrily. "Hello young men, I'm trying to save it. This baby slipped and fell into the water. I think his leg is caught onto something in the water," replied the man getting into the light blue lake. The aliens approached and analyzed the situation better. The farmer was right, he was trying to help. The baby sheep's leg was caught in the seaweed. They saw him struggling into the water, trying to free the baby sheep's leg, always taking care not to hurt the animal. "I'm going to get you out of here, darling," said the farmer petting the sheep. The aliens interfered and helped the farmer. The baby sheep ran happily to his mother, jumping around the meadow with joy. All the other sheep looked happy, and well feed.

"Thank you, young men. You made a young sheep and an old man happy," said the farmer, "Let me give a little cheese in return for your favor." They took the cheese and said their goodbyes, but the aliens hid and stayed a little more to watch the man. He was carefully taking care of each animal, petting, feeding, and talking to each of them. They were impressed by how beautiful everything looked there, even the sky looked bluer and the grass greener. After this event, they both decided something needs to change in their plans. As soon as they got back on board their ship, they told the others the story.

"I think that we should keep the animal lovers alive," said one of them, "The love and the care that farmer had for his sheep is something the Earth needs," he added. "We saw some animal lovers in the city too," added another alien, "Our troop was sent to a big city, and we visited some parks. We saw people walking their dogs, petting them and they were nice to us too." "I understand what you're saying. I'll spend the night watching some animal lovers around the world. I'll try to find out about them and their values in life. I'll go tomorrow to that shit whole planet and check them myself. After some time there I will give you my decision," said the head of the operation. The night passed quickly and the decision did come as quick as the morning did. Everyone gathered in their meeting room and waited for the boss's decision.

"Last night, I made a decision, but I have to go to Earth first. I don't want to make such a big decision overnight. This could change everything," he said. Everyone agreed to the decision, so the last preparations needed continued. The last week was tense and scary for all of them. They had never done something like this before, but they trusted their boss and his judgment. The head of the operation was now on Earth, so he decided to go straight to that exact farmer. He teleported somewhere next to the man's farm. He saw the farmer feeding the sheep, telling them a story, and laughing.

"Hello farmer, I got lost around here," said the alien. "Hello dear, the road is there," said the farmer pointing to a direction, "Walk 10 km, and you'll find the road."

"Thank you so much, farmer. You have some very beautiful sheep, and they are very well-behaved," said the alien trying to catch the farmer saying something wrong, "Did you beat them sometimes? Like parents do to their children?"

"You know sir when you take care of your animals, they take care of you back," said the farmer, "I never hit any of my animals, I don't have any right," added the man. The alien started walking in the direction the farmer pointed, and when the farmer couldn't see him anymore, he teleported into another part of the world. He interacted with a lot of people, with people who had cats, dogs, and even snakes, and he loved them all. He also visited parks and shelters, and everything melted and broke his heart at the same time.

Before nightfall, he teleported back to the ship and called a meeting. "All of you were right indeed. As I wandered the Earth today, I decided that the animal lovers deserved to be saved. I think that the love they have for other creatures is a sign that they could help the Earth get better," he said, "They are the only ones we have a chance with." They aliens decided to all attack at the same times even though they were still confused that all the times were different. They attacked at the same time in all parts of the Earth.

They landed their ships and took everyone hostage. They gave everyone the chance to explain why they did what they did. Unfortunately, most people didn't regret or understand why their actions were bad. But most didn't care and started fighting back again. The aliens still choose a quick and painless death for everyone. Two days after the attack the Earth was different. The people that remained were in shock, still not believing what happened. Some elderly seen war before and knew something was going to happen. "We have to take care of deem kids?" Asked one man.

"Yes, but we'll help you. We want to help you make the Earth a better place for the new generations, help them not make the same mistakes as their ancestors," replied the head of the operation. "But why? Why did you do this?" Asked the man.

"After so many years of humans trying to contact us, we decided to find out what your planet is about nowadays. Every time another planet tries to contact us, we check them, just to be sure everything's alright. In your case, we were shocked," said one alien walking around the crowd. "Our ancestors came to Earth thousands of years ago, they wrote about it, so we knew about your planet. The difference between the planet our ancestors wrote about and your planet now were enormous, so we started watching you," added the alien.

They explained why they decided to attack and how they planned everything. They told them about the farmer that saved the life of the animal lovers, and everything else that happened in the last week. They started planting trees, taking down blocks, and destroying factories. They took all the animals that were in zoos back where they belong. They cleaned the garbage in the seas and oceans and destroyed a lot of cars.

"We'll always be one call away, and we'll always be ready to help. Some of our people will stay here with you, help you with anything you need," said the alien boss. It was hard for the people to get used to this new world because everything was different. A few months after the invasion, the Earth started to heal. The animals would come out of the woods, birds started flying and singing around more than ever, and even the water tastes different. "Even breathing feels diverse, the air has a unique taste now," said one man. "I feel that too. Everything that happened was shocking and crazy, but maybe it's for the best. Our planet can heal now," replied a woman.

Hobbies

For years I had went through the same routine in my life where I would come home from work miserable. The only thing that seemed to bring any joy into my life was on my days off when I would do woodworking. It made me happy and forgets about the horrible week I had at work with my boss breathing down my neck and horrible clients. My friend saw how good I was getting at my hobby and asked me if I hated my job so much and loved woodworking why didn't I turn that into a business.

I never thought of that before and honestly didn't even think that I was capable of starting a business. I knew nothing about it and thought that only rich people that had fancy degrees could go and start a business. I wanted to give it a try though because if I could have my job is something that I love as a hobby than maybe I would feel better. I remembered an old saying that if you do what you love you will never work a day in your life. The first thing I knew is that I had to start small and see if there was even a market for what I was doing.

I created an online advertisement for custom woodworking jobs, and I actually ended up finding a few people interested. I still had my normal job but on the weekends I could create wonderful projects for these people and see the look of joy on their face. When I got money for that it almost felt like free money falling into my lap. I was getting more orders and it got to the point that I was doing woodworking every single day after work. The weekend wasn't enough to keep up with the demand.

My friend helped me design my very own website where people could put in requests for orders and even see reviews that other customers had left. It took a long time but eventually I was making enough money from my woodworking that I was able to quit the job that I hated and start doing my business full time. Since I was working out of my garage all the money that didn't go to materials ended up just being profit. I was starting to wake up excited about work instead of dreading it and wanting to go back to sleep.

It took about a year before I purchased my first actual building that was going to be my shop. I loved my creative freedom and people came to me because they could get any custom piece they wanted instead of having to just buy things that were premade at a store or in some factory. I was worth it to them and when they ask me why I wanted to do this for a living I was honest with them. It had been a hobby as long as I could remember and once I found out I could turn it into a business I would have been stupid to not do it.

https://www.etsy.com/shop/Tedzells

Discount code: books

10% Off Order

Mis abuelos

Mis dudas comenzaron durante una mañana muy mundana. Ese sábado no tenía mucho de extraordinario; comenzó con el café amargo y humeante que contrastaba con la brisa fría del alba veraniego, y un cielo naciente de tono azul pálido que daría paso a los tintes amarillos del amanecer. Durante la tarde, decidí visitar a mis abuelos. Habían pasado algunos días desde la última vez que fui a verlos. Esa decisión hizo que ese sábado dejase de ser mundano.

Estando a pocos metros de llegar a la casa, salió por la puerta un hombre que no recordaba haber visto jamás. De hecho, tampoco se veía como los amigos de mis abuelos, que siempre derrochaban elegancia y un gusto muy refinado. Este hombre vestía diferente. Pero, lo que me hizo esperar a que se subiera al auto antes de acercarme al patio no fue su aspecto, sino su mirada tan extraña.

Me había visto. Clavó sus ojos en los míos… y ese par de irises transmitían un vacío más profundo que el de un hoyo negro en el espacio. Su mirada era opaca, pesada, enojada. Cuando finalmente se fue, tuve el coraje para de acercarme a la puerta y tocar el timbre. Mi abuela Janet abrió la puerta, y me recibió con la misma sonrisa de siempre, y el mismo abrazo apretujado tan característico de ella. El televisor de la sala transmitía una noticia:

"En las calles del suroeste de Texas City, las bandas violentas están fuera de control, traficando con drogas, robando a los negocios y protegiendo su territorio a toda costa. Para un antiguo miembro,

cada día se reduce a dos simples preguntas: ¿Tendré

que matar? ¿Me matarán?".

¡Pasa cariño! ¿Quieres té y galletas? ¿O se te

antoja tomar otra cosa? Té y galletas estará bien,

gracias abuela. Me percaté de que mi abuelo no

estaba en su sillón de la sala, como era lo habitual.

¿Dónde está el abuelo? En la habitación de arriba.

En un momento viene. dicho esto, se fue a la cocina

a preparar la merienda sin titubear una palabra más.

Su respuesta había sido un tanto hermética, pero

viendo que no quiso entrar en mucho detalle, preferí

dejarlo pasar.

Pasado un buen rato, después de las galletas

y las tertulias, mi abuelo bajó. Llevaba puesto

pantalón, camisa y zapatos de vestir, y también un

accesorio un tanto peculiar: un rosario de color negro, y una cruz más pequeña de color negro también. Parecía estar envuelto por un halo de misterio.

Al verme, su rostro se iluminó, y me regaló una de sus maravillosas sonrisas. -¡Qué bueno tenerte por aquí! Pero tendrás que disculparme hoy, tengo que irme. Te debo un helado. - dicho esto, besó mi mejilla y se fue sin más explicaciones. Esa noche no dormí. La curiosidad me carcomía, y llegada la medianoche, me venció. Decidí investigar qué significaban esos collares negros, y descubrí algo sumamente inesperado.

En muchos barrios de la ciudad, hombres jóvenes usaban pañuelos, rosarios y cruces negros para identificarse como miembros de la banda de

Los Cholos. Los noticieros solo podían decir cosas terribles al respecto. "Los jóvenes son pandilleros, miembros de bandas callejeras del barrio como los Cholos. Según la policía, son viciosos, criminales de carrera tatuados, sus vidas están dedicadas a las navajas, cuchillos y pistolas. Roban regularmente a personas inocentes que viven en los complejos de apartamentos.

Roban coches y entran en negocios. Trafican con drogas en las esquinas. Y están constantemente en guerra entre ellos, peleando, mutilando, matando y muriendo por sus territorios, sus colores y sus signos de mano, que tienen un significado especial sólo para ellos." ¿Podría mi abuelo estar involucrado en algo como eso? ¿Por qué? A esta edad...

¿O sería que está involucrado desde mucho antes y nadie lo sabía? Sin importar de qué fuera todo este asunto, iba a descubrir la verdad. Durante las vacaciones de la universidad, comencé a visitar la casa de mis abuelos de forma más frecuente. Esperaba a que llegara la hora de la siesta para husmear por toda la casa. El primer día, corrí a revisar la oficina de cabo a rabo. Revisé cada libro de la biblioteca, detrás de los cuadros, muebles, gavetas, y tras cuatro días de una búsqueda extenuante, no encontré nada.

Había visto casi todos los rincones de la casa donde alguien podría ocultar unos secretos, pero no lograba encontrar nada. Así que pensé, por alguna razón, en la oficina del taller de corte y confección de mi abuela. Un día le pregunté si podía ir con ella al trabajo y pareció maravillada. La última vez que había hecho esto, era una niña pequeña.

A pesar de que me había puesto la misión de desenterrar el misterio en el que mis abuelos parecían estar envueltos, la verdad es que una parte de mi estaba disfrutando todo este tiempo que he pasado con ellos. Los consejos que me han dado y las cosas que he aprendido de ellos este verano, serán tesoros invaluables de mi memoria.

Disfruté el día en el taller, pero tampoco encontré nada allí. Ni una pieza de evidencia que mostrara nexos entre ellos y esa pandilla. A estas alturas, no sabía si darme por vencida o si sentirme aliviada de no haber podido encontrar nada. Podría haberse tratado de un malentendido. Tal vez solo fueron puras casualidades, malas pasadas de la vida o las burlas que esta a veces te lanza porque ¿qué sería la vida sin un poco de humor y de chispa? Me olvidé del asunto por algunos días. Seguí yendo a ver a mis abuelos porque me encantaba estar con ellos.

Un día, estando en la cocina con mi abuela, abrí un gabinete y allí estaba, como el cáliz del Rey Arturo, emitiendo un brillo dorado que podría haber cegado mis ojos. Una caja negra, no muy grande, sin adornos ni nada llamativo. ¿Por qué llamó mi atención? Por el simple hecho de haber estado buscando algo.

Es probable que, en otras circunstancias, esa caja hubiese pasado desapercibida, pero no era el caso. Tuve que esperar el momento preciso para poder revisar esa caja sin que ellos supieran, y cuando por fin pude hacerlo, mis miedos se

materializaron frente a mis ojos. La caja tenía una

pistola cargada, algo de dinero y un trozo de papel

con coordenadas de algún sitio al que yo tendría que

ir para saber qué estaba ocurriendo.

Pero antes, necesitaba vigilar a mi abuelo.

Un día, me escondí en un arbusto cerca de su casa,

esperando a que saliera para seguirlo. Ese día estaba

vestido como siempre lo he recordado: elegante de

pies a cabeza y con una gabardina negra.

Mientras lo seguía, el corazón me latía de

forma descontrolada. No podía dejar de pensar. Mi

mente iba a millones de pensamientos por segundos,

y eso dificultaba mi concentración. Cuando

finalmente llegó al sitio, me di cuenta de que era un

simple parque, común y corriente.

Yo misma había visitado ese parque muchas

veces. Tenía zonas infantiles, y en algunas partes,

mesas de cartas y ajedrez. Mi abuelo fue directo a

las mesas de ajedrez, y se sentó solo, a leer el

periódico. Pasados unos diez minutos, llegó alguien

más a su mesa. Era un hombre un tanto más joven

que mi abuelo, pero con el mismo gusto para vestir.

Se saludaron con un apretón de manos, y el

hombre sacó unas fichas de ajedrez de su maletín.

¿De eso se trataba esto? ¿Una simple partida de

ajedrez? Mi mente sabía que no. Que tras esa

partida algo más se escondía. Por momentos,

hablaban mientras jugaban. Intenté acercarme más

para poder escuchar la conversa, pero no había

arbustos o algo con qué esconderme cerca de esas

mesas, así que tuve que conformarme con solo

poder contemplar la escena a lo lejos.

Aunque no podía escucharlos, estaba segura de que la plática era interesante. Había momentos de silencio muy intensos, miradas inquietantes, como si estuvieran diciendo algo que no podían decir con palabras.

La partida finalmente acabó. Mi abuelo se levantó de la mesa, dio su apretón de mano correspondiente para despedirse, pero me di cuenta de algo. Había dejado su maletín bajo la mesa. Sabía que no se trataba de un simple juego. ¿Qué tenía ese maletín? ¿Quién era ese hombre? Ya era la segunda persona desconocida que estaba con mi abuelo en cuestión de pocas semanas.

Lo que nunca vi venir, es que había alguien más observándome a mí, como un depredador cazando a su víctima. Sus pasos eran de sumo sigilo. Nunca lo escuché, ni vi siquiera su sombra. Simplemente no tuve forma de saber que yo también estaba siendo seguida. Me enteraría pocas horas después.

Regresé del parque llena de incertidumbres, pero decidida a continuar. Ya había llegado demasiado lejos. Busqué las coordenadas para saber a qué dirección tendría que ir ahora, y me topé con un terreno casi desconocido por el mapa. Sin fotos, nombres, edificios, o algún vestigio de vida humana.

Aunque una parte de mi deseaba ir al sitio, mi parte racional sabía que no era tan simple. No podía simplemente ir a un sitio desconocido, baldío y sin nadie que me acompañase. No sabía qué clase de cosas podrían esperarme allí.

Intenté estudiar mis opciones hasta el cansancio, pero mi mente parecía incapaz de formular alguna idea coherente, o que fuese por lo menos suficiente para dejarme salir con vida de ese lugar. Pasadas algunas horas de la madrugada, comprendí que solo me quedaba una opción lógica y viable: confesarle a mi abuelo todo lo que había estado ocurriendo estas últimas semanas.

La idea de pensar que, de ocurrir una tragedia, yo podría haberla evitado en lugar de quedarme en silencio me inquietaba. No podía dejar que algo le pasara a mi abuelo. Esa mañana, me dirigía a contarles todo lo que había sucedido, cuando de repente, sentí un pinchazo. No tuve tiempo de voltear, pues todo me daba vueltas y caí de rodillas al suelo. Mi visión comenzó a oscurecerse, hasta que todo se volvió un vacío

negro. Lo último que recuerdo fue sentir que
levitaba del suelo. Era porque me estaban cargando.

Cuando desperté, no supe dónde estaba, mucho
menos el día y la hora. No estaba amarrada,
encadenada ni vi signos de maltrato o abusos en mi
cuerpo, o al menos es lo que parecía a primera vista.
El lugar no era un sótano o una selva: estaba en una
habitación con muebles de lujo, aire acondicionado
y buena iluminación.

Si esto era un secuestro, es por mucho
diferente a lo que habría esperado. Finalmente está
consciente, señorita Bentley. Voltee en dirección de
la voz que me había llamado por mi apellido. Era el
mismo hombre con el que mi abuelo había jugado
ajedrez en el parque. ¿Quién es usted, y por qué
estoy aquí?

No se preocupe. Responderé a todas sus

dudas, pero necesito que permanezca calmada.

Imagino debe tener sed, aquí tiene una botella de

agua. -Sí que quería el agua, pero no podía fiarme.

Si realmente su vida estuviese en peligro, Bentley,

le aseguro que sus circunstancias en este momento

serían muy diferentes. Puede tomar el agua. Ahora

escuche con atención. Usted está aquí porque puso

en riesgo una misión de vital importancia, en la que

hemos trabajado por mucho tiempo.

¿Una... misión? ¿Dónde estoy? En un

cuartel del FBI, señorita. Su abuelo, el señor

William Bentley, ha estado colaborando con

nosotros por largo tiempo. Reconozco su valentía,

no cualquiera se aventuraría de la forma en que

usted lo ha hecho, pero hemos tenido que detenerla

a como diera lugar, o pondría en riesgo no solo la misión, sino vidas, incluyendo la de su familia.

No supe qué responder en ese momento. En mi mente, había sitio para cualquier tipo de tragedia shakespeariana, pero no para un desenlace como este. Así fue como supe que mi abuelo en realidad no era parte de Los Cholos, sino un colaborador encubierto del FBI.

Wu-Tang Clan

"I don't know how you all see it, but when it comes to the children, Wu-Tang is for the children,"

Ol' Dirty Bastard

O.D.B.

THE END

Old Endeavors

It was Shanice's first day as a college woman at Wayne State University. She never imagined being here but there she is. So while standing there thinking herself. Let's make the best of this. She started walking pointlessly around the campus. She was really amazed by everything. Each new step filled her heart with hope. Shanice have a sense of feeling that could only be described as an "escaping fate." She was really excited and deeply happy. But her face hid it unintentionally. She gave shy looks to other students who were walking around the campus as well. She got some weird looks because of the scars on her face. She didn't mind the looks as a young adult because it is a part of whom she is now.

People always gave her strange looks ever since was in that accident. To Shanice it was her mother's fault. It was the hate that fueled during her teen years. Nonetheless, as a young adult who got accepted into college she knew she shouldn't be mad at her mother any more. But somethings do last forever. Anyways this so-called incident happened back when she was a kid. When she was only seven years old. This event was actually two days before her 8th birthday. Shanice eventually hated her birthdays as well.

Shanice was raised by her single mother Shan and her ghetto ass friends. Although she had some memories of her father back when she was just a baby. He was not in her life. Her mother denied her father was ever around and he was a dead beat. Shanice remembered that her father would call her his "Little Lily" that she loved that more than most. Her mother said that she made things up. Her mother said that she was too young to know remember and was just imagining things. But Shanice remembered her father in a soldier uniform. While her mother kept saying that her father was a douche with various crime records. She remembered those things and her mom denied them all. She was only sure about her father's name. Although her mother loved to refer to him as "Douche" she knew that his name was Jack. And that's all she had for a long time.

But back to March 23, 2012 around one in the morning. It was one of those nights where her mother drove to countless stores that she worked previously to collect money she was owed. Shanice would have to stay in a cold backseat of a worn-out hatchback while holding on to her mom flip phone. "Call the cops if you hear me call your name, Shanny!" her mother would say before she left the car in a hurry. She would wait for an hour or two. Always sitting in the dark doing nothing but worrying about her mother. She got used to it eventually thought; she would daydream about her future. Out of nowhere her mother rushed out of the building and back to the car.

"What's going on, mommy?" with a little concern in her voice.

Her mother didn't answer and started driving, looking backwards with worrying looks. A man rushed out after them, half naked. Then started shouting Shan in the middle of the street. "Come back here! I will kill you, where not finish Shan!"

She was really worried and her mother crazy driving didn't really help. They were going too fast and whenever she asked her to slow down and she wouldn't. Shanice cried a lot within this short time. Just ten to twenty minutes ago she was daydreaming about her upcoming birthday. Maybe her father would make a surprise visit. Maybe they would have some cake? Even some of her friends would have been there to celebrate to. Now she was just worried about their situation and what her mother was doing.

Her mother never calmed down while trying to get away. She got more anxious over time and losing her shit. Whenever she tried to calm her mother, she would get a reaction that was way worse than before. She wanted to stop but her mother was getting worse by every second. Shanice jumped in the front seat trying to hold her mother's hand. That's when her mother actually threw a tantrum an, punched her in her damn head. She wasn't that surprised but they both were shock. Then out of nowhere a tow truck t-boned their car and it flipped over.

She woke up two days later in a hospital. Seeing that the little girl blinks, a nurse rushed to her bed to see if she could speaks. She couldn't really understand her, she needed time to come to her senses. As she was trying to understand what was going on in her head. While still feeling pain all over her body. She had a quick flashback of the things that happened in the car shortly after and she suddenly said with a keen voice,

"Where's mom?"

Then gloominess dismal covered the whole room. Nurses looked at each other, and the doctor looking down at the floor. Then the realization of what happened finally hits her. So in a softer voice….

"I see." and fell back asleep again.

It was her 8th birthday and really wanted her father to be there for her birthday. Instead, she lost her mother now to. After waking up she didn't cry or look worried she just asked for some food. It got everyone in the room so very confused. She was really unresponsive, unreactive to the things that happened around her. She had that dreary look on her eyes that couldn't be bothered. Oh, and a big wound from the car accident that covered half of her face. This was another reason why the doctor and nurse could not stand to looking at her comfortably.

As she was getting better, the hospital used its recourse to give her plastic surgery. Also they suggested that she should talk to a psychiatrist. She heard a nurse say "It's normal that she doesn't say anything for a while. She is all alone in this world right now. She is coming to the realization she became an orphan on her birthday. Can you imagine what it would feel like?" Needless to say, hearing those words didn't really help her and just silenced her more. She was feeling very hopeless about everything at the time including the psychological sessions and having to deal with cps. Many psychiatrists and psychologists tried to reach her, but they all failed as she never, ever spoke back. "You're not even listening, are you?" Was one of the most popular responses she got besides "I know what it feels like?" No, they did not.

However, after a long period of time, a psychiatrist named Pam could actually have her talk for the first time. She had countless therapy sessions with Shanice, and unlike the others, she said "I know that you're listening" and "I am trying to understand you to help you" she liked the attitude and she felt like she could at least try to trust someone. They spent 6 months together, having sessions every other day and dinners on some nights. They discovered in her subconscious memories, apparently her father was in the army. Apparently, being angry at her mother was a natural response. Although she got over quicker than normal. Then after a few more months of medical support, Pam adopted Shanice. Their bond was strong, perhaps stronger than any bond she had in her whole life, although no one would mention that. After hitting puberty they had fights as there would in every other family, they argued about many small things, shouted at each other, but they loved each other in the end.

Although Pam gave her the love she needed the most, she couldn't really shake her steadiness off. She had that draggy eyelids and unresponsive demeanor as an identity at that point. More than a typical teenager. She knew she could go to Pam for anything but it just felt a little different. After starting high school she felt like she was more lost and couldn't figure out what it could be the only thing that came to mind was for her to start reading though some of Pam's therapy books. Although this could of meant, her getting bullied in school by the cool kids. After a while she started reading anything that she could. The pandemic help her with this because she was stuck at home. They had a lot of books back in the house and most of them were psychology books.

She got bullied each day because of her obvious marks on her face. She never understood why things always happened to her. Because of the other school students. But with every page she read Shanice understood more and more. She thought she gets it but will never truly get it. She thought everyone had a story behind them and she thought she might have fun helping other people. Starting with her so-called "bullies" in her high school then eventually figuring out herself.

She succeeded. She talked with them every time they did something to her or someone else. She didn't give any reaction and only tried to get to know them. Even though she knew some of them would turn to violence. She told them that humbly understood them, in a real way. She would tell them that she was always angry too. Many times to be honest it was about nothing. Even though. Beside she never really take it off of other people, it was mainly towards herself. Surprisingly enough, eventually some gave in. some gave up bullying her, but being bullies in general. Then Shanice realized how she could help out other people lives. Is to follow in Pam footsteps and help as many people as she can.

Back to Shanice roaming Wayne State University campus. She was thinking about all her past traumas and other things that led her here. Thinking about being a freshman in a Psychology program made she her smile. She smiled because she knew this was the happiest she had been in a very long time.

My Anxiety Disorder

My morning preparation for work was drawn out longer than usual. On this morning I had to go into work. Of course like every other day, but today was a little different. I faced that problem daily though and meeting new people for me was beyond shyness. Coping with this was my big obstacle when I left the house. I worked in a company where I did not have to face the public, yet I had to meet people on occasion. When interacting with people I would start sweating and my hands would shake. Some people noticed. Others perhaps pretended not to notice so as not to make things worse.

Today I was still parked in the garage, unable to leave the house. I was staring at the steering wheel, holding it with both hands. This particular day I was having a harder time than ever. My boss Bob had asked me to do so negotiation over the phone today. I didn't know how to do that. Nonetheless, that was a part of my new job. But just thinking about it, I was paralyzed even without getting out of the garage. It was still dark, I had gotten up early intending to make this day come to an end as soon as possible. *Come on, Jared, you can do it.* You can get out of this garage. I said to myself tapping the steering wheel, trying to infuse myself with encouragement.

My wife was sleeping, it was so early... Suddenly, I threw my head back feeling frustrated. My anxiety was getting the better of me. I hadn't felt this bad in a long time. I tightened my grip on the steering wheel then closed my eyes. Then I started taking deep breaths over and over again.

This was another attempt to calm myself down and get up the courage to go to work. How was I in this mess? It was just a phone call, a simple phone call. Why does this phone call have me so anxious? I hit the steering wheel twice. I hated this feeling instantly.

When I finally opened my eyes, I was no longer in the car. I was somewhere else, I was at work. Oh, I had finally made up my mind. I was at my desk in my office. I looked around and yes it was indeed my office. Why didn't I remember driving to this place? My anxiety made me forget to do things and made me do them by inertia? I wasn't convinced about that, but I rummaged through the papers on my desk. Yes, it seemed real enough. Then I realized, soon I would have to make that bloody call. Sweat ran all the way down my back just at the thought. Before long my boss would come in and asking when am I making that call. Which I would rather not do. Half an hour had passed and my boss hadn't come in. Would he wait for me to do it without the reminder?

I began to bite my nails fiercely. Seconds later my leg took on a life of its own. It's twitching convulsively, as I sat behind the desk. What should I do now? Then I looked at my computer realizing I didn't have this wallpaper up the other day. When did I change it? I frowned and stopped moving my leg. What is going on here? My head was a hotbed of images that made no sense at all. Were these clothes I had put on this morning? I couldn't say for sure. A shiver ran down my back and spread throughout my body. Something wasn't right. Someone knocked on the door and I jumped out of my chair. I didn't even get a chance to invite person in. As it was my boss and he just opened the door without waiting for an answer. *Jared! We have to go*! Is that what you'll be wearing to the meeting? Well, I recommend a suit. My secretary will get one to you. He said, mysteriously to me.

What are you talking about, Mr. Harrison? I asked, in a shaky voice. Oh my god. Don't you remember I invited you to the meeting with the heads of other companies? It's an important party. My boss reminded me. Hearing those words, my heart stopped. I was forced to punch myself in the chest to get it going again. My boss was cheerful for some reason. What could it possible be about? Besides, what was that about a meeting of the bosses of other companies? It didn't make sense. And why would I have to go? The people there would not know who I am. Sorry, I can't go in to busy. Then boss had left, but I hadn't said a word. I had to reach him and tell him I couldn't do it. Terror gripped me. This party was full of important people... No way. I ran out of my office, screaming at my boss. Imploring him not to make me go. My head was going to explode. I couldn't go to that place. I ran all over the office, there were only the secretaries there at that moment I didn't care about anything else. The only thing I wanted was to get rid of the task that had been imposed on me.

Mr. Harrison, I don't wish to go I can't go..... Mr. Harrisooon!!! The louder I shouted, the more my voice was getting lost in the vastness of the office.

Things were getting so unreal I wandered the halls and Mr. Harrison had disappeared. I was sinking into despair when his secretary intercepted me to hand me the suit for the party. I immediately shouted then she became alarmed. I paid no attention and continued looking for my boss. He was nowhere in the vicinity. I was falling into a spiral of dread. I reached the men's room and took a deep breath. My chest was rising and falling at high speed. I looked in the mirror and panic was painted on my face. I was not going to be any help at this event.

Jared, what are you doing, boy? We've got to get going. Get that suit on!!! Shouted my boss. Who at that moment was coming out of a stall? I jumped again for the second time in a single day. This time out of fright. I had the suit in one hand

and paper towel in the other. My boss rushed me to put it on without giving me time to tell him that I didn't want to go. I changed right there, trying not to collapse. "It won't be so bad, it's a private party, and there won't be many people." I kept repeating to myself. When I came out of the bathroom, my boss was waiting for me. We would go in his car, there I would have the opportunity to tell him I don't want to go, but he forced me into the car.

We are late! said Mr. Harrison.

All the way there, I sweated like a pig. Beads of sweat ran down my face and my hands were so wet that they moistened my pants. My boss didn't seem to mind any of this the fact that I was so anxious, I almost died. Maybe he hadn't noticed the symptoms? I wasn't sure of anything. The only thing that was clear to me was that I was on my way to a party. We were about to arrive, my boss announced. Then everything got exponentially worse. The crisis was coming. I was about to beg him not to take me, but it was too late. He opened the doors, and a crowd appeared. The trembling all over my body made it very clear how bad a time I was having.

Many faces at once looked at me. People dressed in multiple colors with drinks in their hands their eyes fixed on me. My vision blurred, I was not in the capacity to enter that room. I was petrified at the entrance. My boss at my side he walked as if he did not see what state I was in. Even though my boss had already entered, I felt like everyone was still looking at me. A ridiculous amount of time had passed. I could only think that everyone would be laughing at me. At that moment I got dizzy. I felt like I was on the edge of a cliff. I swallowed thickly. Pulling back as I was about to run very far and very fast in the opposite direction.

My boss was no longer there. Everyone was looking at me. Oh no, what kind of nightmare was this? Nausea and fear took over my body. I was going to vomit, then pass out. I wanted to scream for help, for someone to get me out of that place. My voice wouldn't come out. I was in serious trouble.

Out of nowhere my boss was back at my side once again, asking me to come in. We walked in and I felt like someone was watching me closely. My fears returned with an overwhelming clarity. I began to feel short of breath, my tie suddenly was too tight. I reached my hands over to loosen it, but it didn't work. I bent at the waist, gasping for air. Fainting was imminent if the dizziness. Mr. Harrison. I managed to say.

But it was as if we were in different dimensions. He wouldn't listen to me. I raised a hand, asking for help. At that very second many people walked in front and behind me. I was so scared, anxious, terrified... The air did not reach my lungs normally I closed my eyes for a split second to concentrate on not throwing up. Then falling unconscious in the middle of all those people after a little while.

I managed to get out of there and get to safety. I couldn't stand all those looks on me, everyone judging me. It was terrible, what couldn't

I do to get out of there? Would they fire me?
Maybe, but nothing was worse than that. I looked in
all directions. Searching for the exit. As impossible
as it seemed, the entrance had changed places.

Dismay came to me, how was I going to get
out of there if the entrance changed position? Where
were the doors? I was trapped in a party room with
a bunch of people. All which was pointing fingers at
me. While giving me crazy looks. My heart was
hammering in my ribs with enough power to do me
irreparable damage. Unable to help it my legs felt
weak.

My eyes scanned the crowd for the one
person who could get me out of there. At last, I saw
him coming towards me. I finally saw the light at
the end of the tunnel. Get ready, Jared. You will

step up to the podium and give them a thank you speech on behalf of our company. Come on!!! Mr. Harrison said. My boss grabbed my hand and pulled me towards the podium. I did everything in my power to stop him.

My boss without warning exerted unusual force and dragged me to the podium. I was hanging onto his hand, as I screamed at the top of my lungs, NOOOO. My mind was dulled, my nausea increased inhumanly. Then the hair on the back of my neck was so bristling it burned. I twisted with all my willpower to stop myself from going to that podium.

While the others laughed loudly, their eyes were watching me intently. The crowd was pointing their fingers at me while talking to each other. I was so horrified that my screams became uncontrollable. I hit my boss on the arm to make him let me go, while he also laughed with the others. I hit him repeatedly, but he seemed invincible. His laughter could be heard thundering in every corner of the room. We were still at the podium, and my terror was absolute. My hand was numb from my boss's grip and I felt like dying. I lost what little control I had, if it was still there.

My screams were deafening in my head. My blood was boiling in my veins. My boss dragged me away and laughter flooded my ears before I passed out... Then out of nowhere. A hand was shaking my shoulder. I woke up startled and still screaming. NOOOO! It was my wife. Who saw me through my car window. Opened the door and shook me with great force.

Jared, what's wrong? She asked in fright.

They want to force me to give a speech.
Everyone was laughing!!! I screamed and flailed.

Take it easy, that's enough. Calm down. You're not
going anywhere to make a speech. I was reassured
by my wife. It took me a while to realize that it had
all been a nightmare of major proportions. I was
still in my car. However, I was still afraid. It had
been a terrifying experience in that nightmare. The
relief was systematic, but I was never going to
forget that nightmare. It would haunt me for the rest
of my life...

Made in the USA
Monee, IL
05 November 2022

17191213R00064